THE ALIEN FILES

THE ALIEN FILES
#1 CONTACT

BY DANIEL COHEN

AN
APPLE
PAPERBACK

SCHOLASTIC INC.
New York Toronto London Auckland Sidney

ISBN 0-590-76341-5

12 11 10 9 8 7 6 5 4 3 2 1   8 9/9 0 1 2 3/0

Printed in the U.S.A.   40
First Scholastic printing, January 1998

CONTENTS

CHAPTER ONE

1947: The Saucers Arrive

Do you believe in flying saucers?

If you do, you have a lot of company.

Surveys indicate that better than fifty percent of the population of the United States now believes that we have been contacted by alien beings from other worlds. These beings arrive in the vicinity of Earth in round ships commonly called flying saucers, or Unidentified Flying Objects, UFOs (pronounced *yoo ef ohs*).

It is a belief that has been part of American life for over half a century now. Establishment types — scientists, government officials, teachers — tend to ridicule the belief. They say it isn't so. It couldn't happen. But what they say doesn't seem to make much difference to most of us. The belief in flying saucers is still there — stronger than ever.

There has never been anything quite like it in our history.

In order to understand how the idea of flying

saucers has evolved, you have to know where and how it all began.

I can tell you — because I was there.

What can be called the Age of Flying Saucers started in 1947. Oh, there had been rumors of and scares about visitors or invaders from other planets before.

In the latter part of the nineteenth century the eminent American astronomer Percival Lowell was convinced that he had found evidence of an extensive network of canals on the planet Mars. Lowell argued that the canals were of artificial origin and had been constructed by a Martian civilization to irrigate their dry planet with water from the Martian polar ice caps. The theory gained a wide following and hung around until close-up pictures of Mars, taken by probes launched from Earth, proved beyond any shadow of a doubt that there were no canals.

In 1896–1897 there were tales of a "mysterious airship" that had been seen throughout the United States. That was seven years before the Wright brothers' successful flight in 1903. Some people thought the unexplained lights that were being seen in the sky came from a spaceship, not an airship.

A spaceship was said to have crashed in the little town of Aurora, Texas, in 1897. The space alien killed in the crash was supposed to have been buried in the local cemetery. People are still looking for his or her grave.

In 1936 the actor Orson Welles briefly scared an awful lot of people into thinking that Martians had invaded New Jersey with his realistic radio broadcast of the science-fiction classic *The War of the Worlds*.

But nothing that had happened in the past even remotely matched the flying saucer frenzy that began in 1947 — and persists to this day.

Why 1947?

Maybe because 1947 was a very scary year.

A little over a year earlier the United States and its allies had emerged victorious from World War II — the most destructive war in history.

That war ended in 1945 with the introduction of a new and unbelievably terrifying weapon — the Atomic Bomb — that was dropped on the Japanese cities of Hiroshima and Nagasaki by the United States.

Despite the awesome destruction and loss of life caused by the Bomb (it was always capitalized) there was great rejoicing in the United States — at first. It was believed that the superweapon had helped to end the war quickly and saved American lives. And since America was the only country in the world that had the Bomb, no one could challenge it.

That euphoria didn't last long. Almost as soon as World War II was over the United States and western Europe began a long and dangerous confrontation with the former Soviet Union. The period was known as the Cold War. And in 1947 it was really getting cold.

The Soviets didn't have the Bomb, yet, but everyone assumed it was only a matter of time — and not much time — before they got it. East and West would then face each other, each possessing the power to annihilate the other. The next war would not only be worse than the previous war; it could destroy the whole world.

When you have just lived through one total war, another total war seems not only possible, it seems inevitable. There had been World War I, and then World War II, and there would surely be World War III. A whole generation of young Americans grew up at that time sincerely believing that their generation would be the last generation.

And I was one of them.

There wasn't any space program in 1947. There weren't any Earth-orbiting satellites until the Soviets launched one in 1959. But we all knew about the German V-2 rockets that had rained destruction down on London in the final years of World War II. And we knew that rockets were the key to getting into space. For the first time in history space travel was a real and immediate possibility; that is, if we didn't kill ourselves first.

If humans were capable of going into space, it was logical to assume that beings from other, more advanced planets were capable of coming here if they wanted to. And maybe the extraterrestrials would be attracted by what was now happening on Earth. Nuclear explosions on Earth could certainly be detected from space by an alien race possessing advanced technology.

The human race didn't seem capable of saving itself. Perhaps something else from somewhere else would save us. At the very least we would be of more interest to any passing extraterrestrials than we had been before the development of the Bomb. And that is where the flying saucers came in.

Looking back, the spark that set off the flying saucer explosion seems absurdly insignificant. But the atmosphere was so supercharged already, anything could have set it off. It turned out to be the owner of a small fire-extinguisher company.

On Tuesday, June 24, 1947, Kenneth Arnold, a thirty-two-year-old businessman and experienced private pilot, took off from the Chehalis, Washington, airport at about 2 P.M. He was flying his own single-engine plane over the snowcapped Cascade mountain range. He was searching for a lost Marine C-46 transport; a $5,000 reward had been offered for its location.

Arnold had been in the air for about an hour, and was in the vicinity of Mount Rainier when he saw what appeared to be nine brightly illuminated objects flying in a chainlike formation from north to south.

Arnold was an experienced pilot who had flown

in the area many times. He had never seen anything like this before. "The more I observed these objects, the more upset I became," he said. They seemed to be going a lot faster than any known aircraft of that time and, stranger still, they didn't appear to have tails.

One of the objects, the largest, was almost crescent-shaped with a small dome midway between the wingtips. The others were "flat like a pie pan and so shiny they reflected the sun like a mirror."

Their motion through the air was also strange. "Like speedboats in rough water," Arnold said; or in his most memorable phrase, "They flew like a saucer would if you skipped it across the water." Arnold estimated that the sighting lasted two to three minutes and that the objects were a little over twenty miles (thirty kilometers) away.

The words *flying saucer* were originally meant to describe the motion of the objects, not their shape. Indeed, in many of the early sightings objects of a variety of shapes were described. Ultimately the image of a mysterious round craft, a flying saucer, came to dominate the popular imagination. For a while the title *flying disks* was also used, but it never really caught on.

Arnold wrote, "I would have given almost anything that day to have a movie camera with a telephoto lens and from now on I will never be without one."

Later that day when he landed in Pendleton, Oregon, Arnold described his experience to a local newspaper reporter. The story was picked up by the Associated Press news wire and appeared in newspapers and on the radio throughout the United States and in many other countries as well.

It was a slow news day, and oddball stories of this type were often given wide circulation on slow days. Usually they were laughed at and quickly forgotten. That didn't happen to Kenneth Arnold's account. Almost immediately a lot of other people came forward and said, "Hey, I saw those flying saucers, too."

Arnold's first reaction was that he had seen some sort of secret U.S. "jet- or rocket-propelled ship" that was being secretly tested. A more ominous possibility was that he had seen a secret Soviet weapon.

He wanted to know what was going on. "I openly invited an investigation by the Army and the FBI as to the authenticity of my story or a mental and physical examination as to my capabilities. I received no interest from those two important protective forces of our country . . ." At least not for a couple of weeks.

The flying saucer story that now looms so large — the alleged crash of a flying saucer northwest of Roswell, New Mexico, in early July 1947 — looked very different when it happened. The story was in the newspapers and on the radio all over the country, but it was a three-day wonder. Now it has assumed such enormous proportions that it deserves a chapter of its own.

Far more interesting and influential back in 1947 were the sightings of unidentified flying objects by responsible witnesses, like police officers and airline pilots. As time went on the term *unidentified flying object* was used more and more frequently to describe the phenomena. Finally, *Unidentified Flying Object* or *UFO* became the more common phrase, though it never entirely replaced the old *flying saucer*. For those of us serious about the subject, *flying saucer* was too frivolous. *UFO* sounded more serious and scientific.

Typical of the kind of sightings that were reported in this early era is one that took place on July 24, 1948 — just about a year after Arnold's first report. This one was taken very seriously indeed. At about 2:45 in the morning, Eastern Airlines pilot Captain Clarence Chiles looked out the window of his DC-3, which was flying at 5,000 feet (1,500 meters) between Montgomery and Mobile, Alabama. He sighted a dull-red exhaust flame about 700 feet (200 meters) ahead, a little above and to the right of the airliner.

He turned to copilot John Whitted and remarked, "Look, here comes a new Army jet job." Whitted looked out and saw it, too. Later he described it as looking like "one of those fantastic

Flash Gordon rocket ships in the funny papers."

Chiles and Whitted said that the craft was cigar-shaped, and estimated it was about 100 feet (30 meters) long and about twice the diameter of a B-29. It had no wings or fins of any sort. Chiles and Whitted also got the impression that the craft had windows, though they couldn't see any occupants inside.

The thing was only in view for about fifteen seconds, but these were experienced pilots and they got a good look at it. It looked like nothing they had ever seen before. The object was also glimpsed by one passenger who was not sleeping at the time. After it passed the DC-3 the object shot up 500 feet (150 meters) and was lost to view. What was apparently the same object was also reported by a ground maintenance crewman at Robbins Air Force Base in Georgia.

This was the sort of report that really shook people up — particularly in the Air Force, which had been given the task of investigating all those reports of strange objects in the sky. Here were two experienced and responsible pilots, with absolutely no reason to lie, reporting they had seen something that the Air Force knew wasn't a U.S. experimental craft and assumed (and hoped) wasn't a Soviet experimental craft, either. Well, then, what was it?

Later some astronomers suggested that the two pilots had seen a bright meteorite. Chiles and Whitted scoffed at the suggestion. They had been flying for years and had seen all kinds of meteorites during their careers, and meteorites didn't look like that!

People on the ground were seeing things, too. On June 28, 1947, pilots, intelligence officers, and others at Maxwell Air Force Base in Montgomery, Alabama, watched a mysterious bright light streak across the sky, make a sharp right-angle turn, and simply disappear.

The following day at White Sands, New Mexico, Proving Grounds, some rocket scientists saw a silvery disk that they estimated was moving through the sky faster than the speed of sound.

On July 8, 1947, another group of technicians at White Sands were watching a couple of P-82's conducting an ejection-seat test at 20,000 feet (6,000 meters) when a mysterious white, aluminum-looking object suddenly flashed into view. It shot down to ground level, then rose again and disappeared. It made no sound and had no obvious means of propulsion. And on and on and on.

This barely scratches the surface of the reports that were coming in the days, weeks, and months following the Arnold sighting.

In the early sightings suggestions about "secret weapons," either American or Soviet, loom large. But almost immediately another explanation — that these mysterious craft came from beyond Earth — was also being talked about. It was called the "extraterrestrial hypothesis," or "ETH." At first it was assumed that these craft came from some nearby planet, such as Venus or Mars. By the 1960s and 1970s our own probes made the prospect of intelligent life in our solar system seem quite remote. That didn't stifle interest in the ETH one little bit. It merely pushed the place of origin for the alien craft to some distant star or even distant galaxy. The little men didn't come from Mars; they came from Alpha Centauri.

By the end of 1947 the respectable press, such as *The New York Times*, was suggesting that the "hysteria" was over and public interest in flying saucers had fallen off. Perhaps in the editorial offices of the *Times* interest had fallen off, but not in the population at large.

Kenneth Arnold himself complained that while he was being ignored by the authorities and ridiculed by the press he was also being contacted by a lot of ordinary folks who were seeing things in the sky that they could not explain. "I was receiving telephone calls from all parts of the world; and to date I have not received one telephone call or one letter of scoffing or disbelief. The only disbelief that I know of was what was printed in the newspapers.

"I look at this whole affair as not something funny as some people have made it out to be. To me it is mighty serious . . ."

Mr. Arnold, you sure said a mouthful! And, as it has turned out, most people agree with you.

CHAPTER TWO

Roswell!!!

Today you would have to be living in a cave, or some remote province in Mongolia, not to have heard something about Roswell. That's the place in New Mexico where a flying saucer was supposed to have crashed back in the summer of 1947.

But in 1947 you could have blinked and missed it. I didn't miss it, but like practically every other UFO buff, I did forget about it — for years. Decades later the event was reexamined and has now become the biggest UFO story ever.

Here are the basic facts:

On the night of July 2, 1947, there was a violent thunderstorm in the Roswell area. Thunderstorms are common in that part of the southwest during the summer. Mac Brazel, who owned an isolated ranch, heard a crash that was louder and distinctly different from the rumblings of the storm. But he didn't think too much about it — at first.

The following day Brazel and a young neighbor rode out on horseback to check the range. They wanted to see how the cattle were doing and whether some of them should be moved to new fields for grazing. During the ride they found something quite out of the ordinary and totally unexpected.

One of the fields was littered with debris. Most of it looked like dull metal. There were big chunks and little pieces. To the rancher it looked as if something had exploded in the air above the field, and he remembered the loud crash from the previous night. Brazel picked up a couple of the pieces. He found them to be thin — lightweight and flexible — but very strong. He had never seen anything like them before.

Over the next few days Brazel discussed his find with some of his neighbors. They all suspected that it had something to do with the government. There was a big army air base at Roswell, and they figured the army was testing some kind of secret experimental craft and something had gone wrong. All of Brazel's neighbors said it would be a good idea for him to report what he had found.

Still the rancher hesitated. He didn't have a phone, and neither did his neighbors. It would be a three- or four-hour drive to Roswell over bad roads and often no roads at all. The war was over but the country still suffered from wartime shortages. Gas and tires were very expensive and in short supply. Besides, there was lots to do on the ranch, and Brazel felt he couldn't spare the time.

The strange-looking wreckage on the ground would just have to wait.

So it wasn't until July 6 that Mac Brazel actually drove down to Roswell. He told the local sheriff about what he had found, and showed him a couple of pieces of the debris that he had brought with him. The sheriff was puzzled and intrigued. He didn't know what he was looking at and decided to call the nearby air base. A couple of Air Force officers responded almost immediately. They went with Brazel back to his ranch, but it was already dark when they arrived. Examination of the debris field could not begin until the next morning.

So it wasn't until July 7 that Air Force investigators got their first look at the Roswell crash site. There was nothing in the debris that looked familiar to them. In addition to the thin metallic pieces there were light but strong strips that seemed to be made of a woodlike substance. These were covered with symbols — squares, circles, triangles, and less familiar shapes — printed on the surface with a purplish ink.

The Air Force men picked up as much of the material as they could easily carry in their car and headed back to Roswell. Now all of this took place just two weeks after Kenneth Arnold's well-publicized sighting. The papers were full of stories about others who had seen the flying saucers or flying disks. On July 8 Corporal Walter G. Haut, the public relations officer at the base, issued a press release. "The many rumors regarding the flying disk became a reality yesterday when the intelligence office of the 509th Bomb Group of the Eighth Air Force, Roswell Army Air Field, was fortunate enough to gain possession of a disk through the cooperation of one of the local ranchers. . . ."

It went on to say that the material that had been picked up at the Brazel ranch had been sent on to "higher headquarters." That was Eighth Air Force Headquarters in Fort Worth, Texas.

What made this story so potentially intriguing was the place where the flying saucer had apparently crashed. Roswell was home to a large air base where advanced types of military aircraft were presumably being tested. It was also not far from the Atomic Bomb test site at Alamogordo, New Mexico, and the rocket test grounds at White Sands, New Mexico. In the security-haunted world of 1947, that seemed like just the sort of place where flying saucers would be found.

So you can just imagine what sort of sensation the Roswell press release created. One officer recalled that the phone started ringing almost immediately. "I didn't get off the phone until late that afternoon. I had calls from London and Paris and Rome and Hong Kong, that I can remember."

But just as soon as the news got out, the Air Force tried to downplay the sensation it had created. Brigadier General George Ramsey called a press conference at Fort Worth. He said that what had crashed at Roswell was an ordinary weather balloon that must have been damaged in the storm. It was no flying disk and nothing to get all excited about. Photographers took some pictures of Air Force men holding large pieces of a shiny, flexible material that was said to have come from Roswell and had been identified as part of a weather balloon.

At this point, so early in the Age of Flying Saucers, many people still trusted the government. The overpowering atmosphere of suspicion, the fear of conspiracy and cover-up, hadn't really taken over yet. That was still months away. If the Air Force said it was nothing but a downed weather balloon, then that must be what it was. The general public, including those of us who really and truly believed that flying saucers were spaceships from other planets, accepted the weather balloon story.

While people got excited about all sorts of other flying saucer stories, the events at Roswell were forgotten — for years. The massive *Encyclopedia of UFOs*, published in 1980 and probably the most complete book on the subject up to that time, didn't even mention Roswell.

Still the story wasn't completely forgotten. Rumors continually rippled through the world of UFO believers that something really big had happened in the Southwest in the summer of 1947 and that the story was being covered up by the government. But just exactly what happened, and where it happened, was never clear. The name Roswell was rarely, if ever, mentioned.

In 1950 Frank Scully, who had been a writer for the show-business paper *Variety*, published a book called *Behind the Flying Saucers*. He told of three flying saucers that had crashed in 1947 and had been investigated by scientists and officials of the U.S. government.

According to Scully, one of the flying saucers crashed near Phoenix, Arizona, and two others were found in the vicinity of Aztec, New Mexico. Thirty-four humanoid corpses, of small stature, were found in the wreckage. They apparently were Venusians.

The source for all of this amazing information was a mysterious Dr. Gee, "the top magnetic research specialist in the United States." He and a few other top scientists were called in by the U.S. Air Force to examine the saucers, but were supposed to keep quiet about what they had seen. Dr. Gee, however, passed the information on to Silas Newton, an oilman, who in turn passed it on to Frank Scully. Scully's book created a sensation and was the first flying saucer best-seller.

And it was all a complete hoax. Silas Newton and his friend Dr. Gee, really Leo A. GeBauer, were a couple of con men who, among other things, had sold phony oil-well–locating equipment. Whether Scully was fooled by them or was part of the hoax is unknown. But the story really came from the script of an unproduced movie, and the obvious origin of the script was the Roswell incident.

The Scully hoax — and virtually everyone acknowledges that it was a hoax — made a lot of people wary of crashed-saucer stories. Yet they continued to appear in a variety of forms. One persistent rumor was that President Dwight Eisenhower was given a special viewing of the remains of the dead aliens when he visited Edwards Air Force Base in California in 1954.

In 1968 a rumor swept the ufological world that the U.S. government was finally going to reveal all it knew about UFO crashes on a TV documentary. While there was a UFO documentary being prepared by NBC at that time, it certainly did not contain any startling new information.

In all of this, Roswell was never mentioned — until the early 1980s. UFO researchers, going through their old files, ran across the original Roswell report and decided to take a second look at the case. They went back to Roswell to reexamine the facts and interview the surviving witnesses. Suddenly all the rumors of past decades seemed to come together and the name *Roswell* became world famous.

Mac Brazel had died long before the new investigation began. Some of his old friends were still alive and they thought the rancher knew a lot more about what had happened than he ever told publicly. Brazel was normally closemouthed. His friends believed that he had been ordered to keep quiet about what he knew by the Air Force. "In those days," one man recalled, "when the government told you shut up, you shut up." Brazel's friends said that he had become quite bitter about the way he had been treated.

Other people who had lived near Roswell or had been stationed at the base in 1947 believed that the debris that had fallen on the Brazel ranch was only part of the story. They said that apparently an alien spacecraft had been damaged in the July 2 storm, but that only part of it fell on Brazel's property. The main body of the ship crashed a few miles away. According to rumors, the site was immediately sealed by the military.

At the main crash site, so these stories ran, were the bodies of space aliens who had been aboard the ship and were killed in the crash. The bodies were taken to the base hospital at Roswell Air Base and then secretly flown off to some other location. The location most commonly mentioned was the huge Wright-Patterson Air Force Base near Dayton, Ohio. Wright-Patterson was to become the center for Air Force UFO investigation in the months and years to come.

A nurse at Roswell who claimed to have actually seen the bodies of the aliens before they were taken away described them as being a little smaller than adult humans. The head was larger than that of an ordinary human and the eyes were larger still. The hands had only four fingers and the bodies appeared thin and very delicate.

The nurse said that the bodies were immediately frozen, sealed in rubberized mortuary bags, crated, and shipped off. Other witnesses said they had accompanied the mysterious crate to the Wright-Patterson base, after which it seemed to simply disappear.

The bodies, according to several stories, were hidden in freezers in a mysterious and closely guarded Hangar 18. Other stories say that the hangar contained the remains of the downed spaceships, which scientists were studying. None of the really sensational later accounts has been confirmed. Many of them are anonymous or secondhand. They would never stand up in court. But they did catch the public imagination. Suddenly Roswell was back in the news in a very big way. It was the subject of several best-selling books and a made-for-television movie. A slickly produced UFO conspiracy film, *Hangar 18,* was released in 1980. The Roswell story is one of the underlying themes of the enormously popular *X-Files* television series as well as a central part of the blockbuster film *Independence Day.* A documentary that supposedly shows an autopsy being performed on one of the aliens back in the 1940s has been shown widely on television and is a popular sale item in video stores.

The town of Roswell, itself, has become a center of attention. The Roswell Air Base closed down a long time ago, and the town had been in economic decline ever since. Postcards sold in town advertised it as being "in the middle of nowhere," and if you locate it on a map you will find that is a pretty accurate statement. But Roswell has a new industry — UFO tourism. It's now home to two UFO museums and an annual UFO festival. Tourists pay fifteen dollars and more to make a pilgrimage to the spot on the former Brazel ranch where the debris was found. For some, the visit is a religious experience.

All of this new attention finally got to the U.S. Air Force. In September 1994 Air Force officials admitted that their weather balloon story of 1947 was a cover-up — well, sort of a cover-up, anyway. Now they said that what had fallen near Roswell that July was a balloon all right, but not an ordinary weather balloon. They said that this balloon was part of Project Mogul, a secret spy project that used huge balloons to carry sensors high into the atmosphere in an attempt to detect atomic tests that might be conducted in other countries, particularly the Soviet Union. It was the Cold War again. The debris found near Roswell, in this explanation, was a smashed part of one of the balloons: the sensors and — what was most important to the growth of the flying saucer theories — parts of radar reflectors made of metal foil. Since the project was secret back in 1947, the Air Force said it released a cover story about a weather balloon.

Colonel Albert Trakowski, who had run Project Mogul, acknowledged that the new revelation would not end the belief in spaceships or a government cover-up. "People believe what they want to believe," he said. "In New Mexico flying-saucerism has become a minor industry."

Of course he was right. Walter G. Haut, who had written the original flying-disk press release for the Air Force and who is now president of one of the Roswell UFO museums, responded: "All they have done is give us a different kind of balloon. Then it was weather, and now it's Mogul. I don't think anything has changed. Excuse my cynicism, but let's quit playing games."

CHAPTER THREE

What If They Aren't Friendly?

For those of us who, from the very start, suspected that the flying saucers came from another planet, there was only one important question: Were their passengers friendly or unfriendly?

The early evidence seemed to indicate that they weren't friendly.

The ominous news began with what may have been a foolish little hoax that turned into a tragedy. It was an event that cast a long shadow.

A few days after his well-publicized sighting Kenneth Arnold got a letter from a Chicago editor named Raymond A. Palmer. Palmer edited a couple of popular science-fiction magazines and had a great interest in strange phenomena.

Palmer wanted Arnold to write an article about what he had seen. The editor also said that he had heard about a strange experience with a saucer-shaped craft on an island off the coast of Washington State. Would Arnold be willing to investigate the story? After some thought Arnold said he would.

On June 21, 1947, three days before Arnold's sighting, a U.S. Coast Guard launch commanded by Harold A. Dahl was patrolling Puget Sound. On board was Dahl's fifteen-year-old son and the family dog. The boat put in at Maury Island, about three miles (approximately two kilometers) out from Tacoma, Washington.

Suddenly six very large "doughnut-shaped machines" appeared overhead. One of them looked as if it were having some sort of mechanical trouble and began spewing out molten metal fragments. A fragment burned Dahl's son. Another killed the dog.

Dahl reported the events to his superior, Fred Crisman. The next morning a man wearing a dark suit showed up at Dahl's house and warned him, "Silence is the best thing for you and your family. You have seen what you ought not to have seen."

The day after that, June 23, Crisman went out to Maury Island to examine the scene. One of the doughnut-shaped craft appeared, circled the bay, and disappeared into the clouds. Crisman took some photographs, but when they were developed they were covered with white spots "as though they had been exposed to some radiation."

A week later Kenneth Arnold arrived in Tacoma to talk to Dahl and Crisman. What followed was a series of bizarre meetings in Arnold's hotel room, waterfront cafes, and an apparently abandoned building that Dahl said was his office. There were mysterious phone calls and enigmatic statements such as, "Mr. Arnold . . . this flying saucer business is the most complicated thing you ever got mixed up in." The stories that Dahl and Crisman told seemed to change and shift constantly. Arnold began to feel that he was being watched and that his hotel room had been bugged. By now he was thoroughly confused and wishing that he had never taken on this assignment.

Feeling out of his league, Arnold called Lieutenant Frank Brown and Captain William Davidson, a couple of Air Force intelligence officers stationed at Hamilton Army Air Base in California. They had interviewed Arnold after his own sighting and they agreed to fly up to Tacoma and interview Dahl and Crisman. The two men were not overjoyed at the prospect of being interviewed by Air Force intelligence. In fact, Dahl refused to be interviewed and walked out of the room. But Crisman was in Arnold's hotel room when Brown and Davidson arrived. They talked for a few hours, with the intelligence officers becoming increasingly bored and skeptical about what they were hearing. Around midnight the officers announced that they were returning to California immediately. They didn't even want to wait around for a box of the mysterious substance that the flying saucer was supposed to have spewed out over Maury Island.

On the return trip the B-25 carrying Brown and Davidson crashed shortly after takeoff. There were survivors from the crash, but the two intelligence officers were killed. It was rumored that the wreckage of the plane was found to be "radioactive." Everything mysterious was "radioactive" in 1947.

The Tacoma *Times,* which had been following the story, headlined:

SABOTAGE HINTED IN CRASH
OF ARMY BOMBER AT KELSO
Plane May Hold Flying Disk Secret

Badly shaken, Arnold abandoned the investigation and left town. In Chicago Ray Palmer said that he, too, was ending his attempt to probe the "Maury Island mystery." He hinted darkly that he "wanted no more blood on his hands."

An investigation of the crash found no evidence of sabotage or radioactivity. And a closer look at the case indicated a lot of holes in the story told by Crisman and Dahl. They were not members of the Coast Guard. They were a couple of guys who owned an old boat and carted lumber around Tacoma Harbor. Dahl's son had been injured all right, but he was already in the hospital on the day the material from the flying saucer was supposed to have fallen on him. Crisman had been trying to peddle false ideas to Ray Palmer for years, without success, until the Maury Island incident. Palmer himself may have encouraged the hoax.

The government briefly considered prosecuting Dahl, Crisman, and Palmer. But for what? Even if they had caused two intelligence officers to fly to Tacoma on a wild-goose chase, they didn't cause their plane to crash on the return trip. Wisely, the prosecution idea was dropped.

In the end most people, including many of us who thought flying saucers were spaceships, decided that it wasn't the "Maury Island Incident," it was the "Maury Island Hoax."

And yet, it had a lasting impact. A definite note of paranoia had been sounded. The *X-Files* world of evil aliens, mysterious deaths, and government cover-ups had been introduced for the first time — in June 1947. Today there are still those who insist that "something happened" at Maury Island that June day.

There wasn't any doubt about what happened on January 7, 1948, near Fort Knox, Kentucky. Captain Thomas Mantell of the U.S. Air National Guard was killed chasing a flying saucer.

More than any other case in the early history of UFOs, the death of Captain Mantell made people suspect that whatever was out there was downright deadly.

At about 1 P.M. people in the area of Fort Knox

began reporting a large unknown object in the sky. It was white or silvery and looked like "an upside-down ice cream cone" or was "umbrella-shaped."

Officials at nearby Godman Air Force Base asked a flight of four National Guard F-51's, which were in the vicinity, to investigate.

The planes closed in on the object. One pilot described it as "round like a teardrop, and at times almost fluid."

Three of the planes abandoned the chase after a few minutes. The flight leader, Captain Thomas Mantell, decided to go after the object. He radioed the Godman tower: "I'm closing in now to take a good look. It's directly ahead of me and still moving at about half my speed . . . the thing looks metallic and of tremendous size . . .

"It's going up now and forward as fast as I am . . . that's about 369 m.p.h. (590 km.p.h.) I'm going up to 20,000 feet (6,000 meters), and if I'm no closer, I'll abandon chase."

The time was 3:15 P.M.

That was the last radio contact made with Mantell.

Later that day Mantell's decapitated body was found in the wreckage of his plane on a farm near Fort Knox. His watch had stopped at 3:18 P.M., which was assumed to be the time of impact.

There were the usual stories that the wreckage of the plane was riddled with bullet holes and that it was radioactive. This was denied by crash investigators.

The almost-certain reason for Captain Mantell's death was that he had blacked out from lack of oxygen. The plane carried no oxygen system. The engine itself may have died of oxygen starvation, causing the plane to crash.

So we know what killed Captain Mantell. The question remains, what was he chasing?

The first explanation offered was that he was chasing the planet Venus. That explanation is not as foolish as it sounds. At certain times and under the right atmospheric conditions Venus can appear huge, and many people, including experienced pilots, have been fooled into thinking it was something else. The problem with the explanation in this case is that Venus would not have been visible at all at the time and place of Mantell's encounter. The Air Force was left struggling for another explanation. The general public became more and more skeptical . . . and uneasy.

In this case there was an explanation — but it was secret. The U.S. government was using gigantic *skyhook* weather balloons to collect information about the upper atmosphere. A skyhook balloon expanded to a diameter of 100 feet (30 meters) and, if caught in a jet-stream wind, could move along at nearly 200 m.p.h. (320 km.p.h.) These balloons looked a lot like the "teardrop" and "upside-down ice cream cones" described by witnesses in Kentucky. In 1948, with many wartime security regulations still in effect, the skyhook project was classified. It was secret. Those who knew about it couldn't talk about it.

If Captain Mantell had known about skyhook balloons he probably wouldn't have lost his life trying to chase one. If military authorities could have talked about the balloons, they wouldn't have sounded so downright evasive when trying to explain what Mantell had been chasing. By the time the skyhook project was declassified it was too late. A lot of us just wouldn't trust an official explanation anymore.

On the night of October 1, 1948, Lieutenant George F. Gorman of the North Dakota Air National Guard was returning to the airport in Fargo in his F-51.

As he was preparing to land, the airport tower told him there was a piper cub, a small plane, in the area and that he should watch out for it. Gorman spotted the Piper Cub about 500 feet (150 meters) below him. He also saw what appeared to be the taillight of another plane to his right. The tower insisted that they knew of no other plane in the area. Gorman decided to investigate.

He closed in to about 1,000 yards (900 meters), and suddenly the light veered sharply to the left.

Gorman reported, "I put my F-51 into a sharp turn and tried to cut off the light in its turn. By that time we were at about 7,000 feet (21,000 meters). Suddenly it made a sharp right turn and we were headed straight at each other. Just when we were about to collide I guess I got scared. I went into a dive and the light passed over my canopy at about 500 feet (150 meters). Then, it made a left circle at about 1,000 feet (300 meters) above, and I gave chase again."

These maneuvers continued for a while. Then the object came at him again. When collision seemed imminent it suddenly shot straight up into the air and disappeared. Gorman tried to follow, but his plane went into a power stall and he lost sight of the light. The aerial dogfight was over; it had lasted nearly half an hour.

Gorman was a veteran pilot and had been a flying instructor during the war. Yet this encounter left him so rattled that he had great difficulty landing his plane. When he described the encounter to his commander at the base, he said that he was convinced that "there was thought" behind the maneuvers.

Two of the air traffic controllers in the tower saw the light heading off to the northwest at a great rate of speed. The pilot of the Piper Cub also saw the light.

Air Force investigators theorized that Gorman had been chasing some sort of lighted balloon. The problem with this explanation was that balloons can't behave the way the light did.

The Gorman dogfight received a great deal of publicity and became one more addition to the growing "unidentified" file.

Here was another example of an experienced pilot seeing something that couldn't or shouldn't be there. No one in authority could or would adequately explain what it was. And whatever it was, it didn't act friendly.

Is it any wonder that a lot of us began to believe that if the earth wasn't actually under attack, it was certainly under hostile observation?

CHAPTER FOUR

The Space People

Have you ever seen the great, old science-fiction classic film *The Day the Earth Stood Still*? It was made in 1951.

A big, silvery flying saucer lands right smack in the middle of Washington, D.C. Out steps Klaatu, a very human-looking space alien played by Michael Rennie. He is on a mission to try and make peace in a world threatened by nuclear war. But the world's leaders will not listen. Poor Klaatu must rely on his gigantic and superpowerful robot Gort to scare the warlike nations.

In the deep Cold War days of the early 1950s that message resonated. So did the flying saucer.

All science fiction, you say. Not back in the 1950s. On November 20, 1952, a man named George Adamski said that a flying saucer landed on a hill in the middle of the California desert. Out stepped Orthon, a handsome, smooth-faced Venusian with shoulder-length blond hair, wearing what looked like a ski suit with a broad belt around his waist.

Orthon communicated with Adamski telepathically. He said that the "Space People" had come in friendship because they were deeply concerned about "radiations from our nuclear tests." The Venusian insisted that the people of Earth had better begin living according to the laws of the "Creator of All" or this planet might not survive. After about an hour of telepathic conversation Orthon returned to his flying saucer and flew off.

This contact with a space alien was allegedly witnessed by six other people who later signed sworn statements to that effect.

The 1952 contact in the desert wasn't Adamski's first experience with flying saucers. He said that he first saw the ships over his home in Palomar Gardens, California, in August 1947. There had been other flyovers of his home, and his "space friends" had already communicated telepathically with him. They directed him to the desert in 1952 for the face-to-face meeting.

After this first face-to-face meeting, many other contacts were to follow. These included rides on spaceships and long dialogues with Firkon, a Martian, and Ramu, a Saturnian.

Adamski's own background is murky. He often referred to himself as "Professor," though, as far as anyone has been able to determine, he was never a professor of anything. In fact, when he started telling his stories he was working the grill in a hamburger stand on the road to Mt. Palomar Observatory in California. It was sometimes hinted that he was an astronomer at the famous observatory, but he wasn't.

George Adamski wasn't your average fry-cook. He had a long-standing interest in occultism and mystic philosophy. He had even conducted small classes in esoteric subjects. What he said then sounded an awful lot like the philosophy he later attributed to the space people.

Adamski had also written *An Imaginary Trip to the Moon, Venus and Mars,* an unpublished book of science fiction. Later he offered a revised version of the manuscript as a factual account of his contact experiences.

To those who scoffed at his stories and called him a liar, George Adamski offered other proof. He had what he said were a series of pictures that he had taken of the spaceships he encountered. The most famous of these pictures, supposedly the picture of a round "scout ship" photographed as it took off, looked suspiciously like the sort of heat lamp once used in chicken incubators. No matter — it became one of the most celebrated flying saucer pictures of the era.

With all the doubts that had been raised about Adamski's stories you might think that no one would pay any attention to him. But if you thought that, you would be dead wrong. Adamski was a charming and persuasive man and he became extremely famous. Though many ridiculed him, he also picked up lots of followers. He was in great demand for lectures, radio and TV appearances, as well as countless interviews for newspapers and magazines. He toured the world, speaking to millions. He even claimed to have held private audiences with Queen Juliana of the Netherlands and Pope John XXIII, though these stories are as hard to confirm as his conversations with Firkon and Ramu.

When he died in 1965 he was still a celebrity. Some of his followers continued to operate a George Adamski Foundation out of California for years. Most significantly, Adamski's success inspired a whole host of other individuals to come forward who claimed that they, too, had been in touch with the Space People. These were the *contactees*, the radical fringe of the flying saucer world.

Dr. Daniel Fry was apparently working for an aerospace company at White Sands Proving Grounds in New Mexico when he had his encounter with the Space People. It was July 4, 1950, and through a series of minor mishaps Fry found himself stranded at a deserted camp at White Sands in the middle of the desert. In the evening, when it got cooler, he decided to go out for a walk. As he was walking, an "object" came out of the sky and landed quite near him. "I could see that its shape was an oblate spheroid about thirty feet (nine meters) in diameter at the equator or largest part." It was, he soon discovered, a spaceship.

"A closer inspection showed that the highly polished metal surface was silvery in color, with a slight violet iridescence."

Fry reached out to touch the thing, and suddenly a voice that came out of thin air said, "Better not touch the hull, pal, it's still hot."

Fry was so startled that he fell over backward and sprawled in the sand. The voice said, "Take it easy, pal, you're among friends."

The friend turned out to be a spaceman named A-Lan, or more simply, Alan. Alan hadn't actually landed in the spaceship, but was "broadcasting" from a "mother ship" far out in space.

This was no random contact. Fry had been specially chosen. "We have carefully investigated the minds of many of your top scientists. In every case we found that their minds had hardened into a mold based on their present conceptions. Their minds have advanced to an extent where they believe they know almost everything in the scientific world. So they find it difficult to change their minds or form new opinions."

Fry, it seems, was open-minded, a true seeker of knowledge. He was to carry the message of the Space People to Earth. The message was that "political tensions, which now exist between the many nations of Earth, must be eased," otherwise there was likely to be a "war of extermination."

One of the more startling things that Fry was told was that Alan's ancestors originated on Earth. They had fled to Mars to escape the destruction of a total war, which devastated an earlier earthly civilization. Naturally they kept the home planet under observation and had returned to Earth to keep the present generation of humans from repeating the mistakes of the past.

To prove their powers the Space People took Fry on a little ride from White Sands to New York and back. The trip took about thirty minutes. Fry figured they were going 8,000 m.p.h. (12,900 km.p.h.).

Alan departed with the words: "Good-bye, Dan. Do your best. Help people understand the truth about themselves, their existence, and their future. When you have made enough progress, we will contact you again."

Fry's tale of the Space People who had come to Earth to save us from ourselves was a message people wanted to hear. He was, briefly, the most well-publicized contactee in the country. He appeared on radio and television, gave newspaper interviews and lectures, even wrote a popular book. And then he made a big mistake. He agreed to take a lie detector test on a popular West Coast TV show — and he flunked.

Howard Menger, a sign painter from New Jersey, was probably the most famous contactee on the

East Coast. He added a new dimension to the tales by claiming that he had been contacted repeatedly since he was a child. He said the contacts began in 1932, when he was only ten years old. While he was playing in the woods near his home in New Jersey he came upon a beautiful golden-haired woman in the woods.

"She was the most exquisite woman my young eyes had ever beheld! The warm sunlight cascaded around her face and shoulders. The curves of her lovely body were delicately contoured . . ."

The woman said, "Howard, I have come a long way to see you and talk with you." He was told that he would be contacted again when he was old enough to understand the teachings of the Space People and what would be expected of him as a messenger of the Space People.

According to Menger there were other meetings — loads of them over the years. Among the things revealed to Menger in these meetings was that he and his second wife, Connie, were reincarnated from previous lives on the planet Venus. Menger produced a fantastic collection of photographs of spaceships and their occupants. Unfortunately all of the photos — every single one — were so fuzzy and out of focus that it was quite impossible to tell what was being shown. You had to take Menger's word that the dark shape in the foreground really was a Venusian.

Menger and other contactees, like the fellow

who called himself the Mystic Barber and wore a wire coat hanger strapped around his head to use as an antenna to pick up messages from the Space People, were regulars on late-night radio talk shows in New York City. They would enthrall hordes of teenage boys, who stayed up well past their bedtimes to hear them spin their exotic tales, and perhaps to dream that they, too, might someday meet that golden-haired woman in the woods.

Back out in California, contactee Gabriel Green took another approach. He went political. He claimed to have had hundreds of flying saucer sightings and to have been contacted in person by beings from many different planets. Among them were travelers from Venus, Mars, Saturn, Alpha Centauri, and Coma Berenices.

In 1960 Gabe was asked by the Space People to run for political office in an effort to "plant the seeds of needed reform in our world." He became an independent candidate for president of the United States, but withdrew and threw his support to John F. Kennedy. During his short-lived campaign Gabe promised all sorts of things, like ending traffic jams on California freeways and telling the people the "truth" rather than keeping them in "planned ignorance of the most vital information in history." Another important part of Green's platform was opposition to nuclear testing.

In 1962 Gabriel Green ran for the U.S. Senate

in California and actually collected over 171,000 votes in the Democratic primary. In 1972 he was again running for president, this time on the Universal Party ticket. His running mate was another contactee, Dr. Daniel Fry.

Green said that he was a "vocal telepathic channel for the Space Masters and the Great White Brotherhood — the Spiritual Hierarchy of Earth." He also claimed that he "acted as a channel for energies from the Space People, which enables persons to reexperience their past lives, without hypnosis. Instant telepathy, clairvoyance, time travel, Higher Self-Contact, soul travel to spaceships and other planets are also achieved by this unique awareness-expanding technique."

Gabe's philosophy obviously represented a blending of flying saucer lore with much older occult and mystic beliefs. And he was by no means the wildest one out there.

Those of us on what might have been called the scientific side (or at least the more respectable and sane side) of the ufological world were regularly reduced to a state of sputtering rage by the antics of the contactees. All we were trying to do was tell the world that the spaceships had arrived, and that the government knew it and was covering it up. The contactees said they were riding around in spaceships and talking telepathically to people on Alpha Centauri. And they were telling people on Earth how to recapture their past lives on Atlantis. All of this made the world of UFOs appear as if it were filled with fakers and gibbering loonies.

And yet, silly as all the contactee tales sound today, they struck a responsive chord in the nuclear-haunted world of the time. The contactees attracted thousands, possibly hundreds of thousands, of believers.

And they did more. They made UFOs part of the occult world. Even today, New Agers are just as likely to channel to or get telepathic messages from Space People as they are from the spirits of the dead or the mystic masters of Tibet.

CHAPTER FIVE

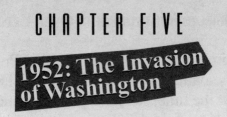

1952: The Invasion of Washington

In July 1952, Washington, D.C., was invaded by flying saucers.

Okay, so it wasn't quite like the 1996 summer blockbuster movie *Independence Day*. The White House wasn't blasted out of existence or anything like that. But flying saucers *were* spotted in restricted airspace over the White House and the Capitol. There was near panic in the control room at Washington National Airport. Commercial aircraft were warned to stay out of the area. Air Force jets were sent up to find the "unknowns" — whatever they were.

Headlines in the Washington press read:

JET FLYERS TOLD TO SHOOT DOWN SAUCERS
THE DAY THE SAUCERS VISITED WASHINGTON, D.C.
JETS LOSE RACE WITH GLOWING GLOBS

And a headline on the front page of *The New York Times* announced:

Captain Edward J. Ruppelt, head of Project Blue Book (the name given the Air Force UFO investigation) at the time, stated: "No flying saucer report in the history of the UFO ever won more world acclaim than the Washington National sightings."

Since 1947 *flying saucers* (still the most commonly used term) have been officially debunked many times. The end of the flying saucer craze had been announced repeatedly. But the reports of strange and unknown lights in the sky kept coming in. Public interest remained high. So did the public suspicion that something was going on that we weren't being told about. The reaction to the events in Washington shouldn't have surprised anybody. But, as usual, it did.

The Washington excitement started late on Saturday night, July 19, 1952. It was the middle of a traditionally awful Washington heat wave. At about 11:40 P.M. the radar at Washington National Airport began detecting strange objects in the sky.

Edward Nugent was the air traffic controller manning the radarscope at the time. Nugent couldn't identify what he was seeing, so he called supervisor Harry Barnes over to look at the scope.

Barnes later described the scene. "Our shift had been on duty about forty minutes. Eight men were on this particular shift. It was a normal night both for flying and weather. The sky was cloudless, no storms were approaching. Air traffic was light as usual for that period . . ."

What Nugent and Barnes saw on the radar scope were seven *pips*, pale violet spots on the screen. They indicated objects in the sky some fifteen miles (about nine and one-half kilometers) south, southwest of Washington. They tracked the seven pips for a few minutes and estimated that they were moving between 100 and 130 m.p.h. (160 and 210 km.p.h.) Barnes described the movements of the objects on the screen as "radical compared to those of ordinary aircraft."

Barnes called over a couple of other air controllers to confirm the observations. He called the airport control tower, and the radar operator verified the sighting.

Then things began to get really interesting. Barnes had some technicians check the radar. They declared it was working perfectly. Puzzled, and more than a little worried about these strange objects that apparently were bearing down on the nation's capital, Barnes called the Air Force.

Barnes expected that the Air Force would immediately send up planes to check the objects — if objects they were. But nothing happened. In the meantime more reports were being received. Some incoming pilots told of seeing unidentified lights in the night sky. Others said they saw nothing out of the ordinary.

Radar operators at Andrews Air Force Base near

Washington picked up the targets. Ground personnel at National Airport reported a "bright orange light" in the sky.

The most impressive report came from Captain S. C. Pierman, a commercial pilot for Capital Airlines. He had just taken off from National Airport when he spotted a "bright light." During the next fifteen minutes he continued to see mysterious lights, at one time as many as six. The lights coincided with the radar observations at the airport. Another pilot approaching National also saw a light off his left wing. This, too, was confirmed by radar personnel on the ground.

Whether the Air Force actually sent any planes up to check on the mysterious sightings and radar readings is still a matter of dispute. Some witnesses said that at about 3 A.M., some three hours after Barnes' first call, radar-equipped jet fighters from a Delaware base roared into the sky. They made several passes over the Washington area but saw nothing. By that time the blips had disappeared from radar screens. Finally, after several passes, the planes ran low on fuel and headed back to base. After they were gone the mysterious blips showed up again, and were detected on and off for another couple of hours. On the other hand, the Air Force vigorously denied that they had ever sent up any planes that day.

Apparently no one bothered to inform Air Force intelligence about the incident; in any case Air

Force intelligence said they never heard anything. No one really believed Air Force intelligence hadn't even heard about what was happening, and that led to headlines such as AIR FORCE WON'T TALK.

The Air Force certainly wasn't talking to Captain Ruppelt of Project Blue Book, who was supposed to be the top U.S. UFO investigator. He was stationed at Wright-Patterson Air Force Base near Dayton, Ohio. Ruppelt found out about the overnight excitement in Washington from his morning newspaper.

He was understandably angry and immediately made arrangements to fly to Washington and make a firsthand evaluation of the situation. He wanted to visit the various airports, the weather bureau, and a number of other locations around the city. When he got to Washington Ruppelt discovered he was stranded. The Air Force wouldn't give him a car to get around the city. Then he was told that he had permission only to visit the Pentagon, and if he went anywhere else he would be disobeying orders. The Air Force said that it was investigating UFOs. It just wouldn't let its top investigator do his job.

Disgusted, Ruppelt caught the next flight back to Dayton, Ohio. "I decided that if saucers were buzzing Pennsylvania Avenue in formation, I couldn't care less."

When Ruppelt got back to Wright-Patterson he

found his desk cluttered with new UFO sighting reports from all over the country. The news from Washington had stimulated a greater interest in UFOs than at any time since the summer of 1947.

And the news from Washington wasn't over yet.

At about 9 P.M. Saturday, July 26, the radar operators at Washington National Airport began seeing those mysterious blips on their screens once again. Barnes was called in and he confirmed that these targets appeared identical to the ones he and others had seen a week earlier. He called the air controllers at Andrews Air Force Base just outside of Washington. They were seeing the same unknown targets as well. Commercial pilots in the vicinity began reporting strange lights in the sky. A United Airlines pilot radioed, "One's here. We got him in sight. He's real pretty."

Barnes and others became increasingly anxious. After all the excitement of the previous week he knew this was a situation airport personnel were not really equipped to handle alone. Within two hours Barnes had called the Pentagon. This time he got action. All civilian aircraft was ordered out of the area. At 11:25, a few minutes after his call, F-94 jet interceptors appeared over Washington.

News of what was going on got around fast. Reporters and photographers flocked to the airport. They were then ordered out of the radar room. They were told that classified radio frequencies and procedures were being used.

The excuse given for clearing the radar room of reporters was sheer nonsense. Ruppelt wrote:

When I later found out that the press had been dismissed on the grounds that the procedures used in an intercept were classified, I knew that was absurd because any ham radio operator worth his salt could build equipment and listen in on any intercept. The real reason for the press dismissal, I learned, was that not a few people in the radar room were positive that this night would be the big night in UFO history — the night when a pilot would close in on a UFO and get a good look at it and they didn't want the press in on it.

That magic moment never arrived. Air Force pilots, with one exception, saw nothing unusual, despite the fact that radar continued to show UFOs in their vicinity. One pilot, however, did report seeing mysterious lights in the sky. He tried to close in on the lights, but they always eluded him.

Even though the definitive close-up saucer sighting had not taken place, this second wave of Washington UFOs created a wave of heightened public interest and near hysteria. The Air Force called a press conference to be conducted by Major General James A. Samford, chief of intelligence. Though the press conference was held in a large briefing room, the Air Force had underestimated interest. The room was crammed to overflowing with reporters and photographers. It was the largest press conference the Air Force had held since the end of World War II.

General Samford did most of the talking. Captain Ruppelt, who was supposed to be the expert, stood in the background, grinding his teeth. The general tried his very best to dismiss the whole phenomenon. He immediately set out to reassure a nervous nation that there was no danger. "There has been no pattern that reveals anything remotely like purpose or remotely like consistency that we can in any way associate with menace to the United States." In short, these things weren't Soviet secret weapons.

Okay, the reporters wondered, if the things weren't dangerous, and didn't come from Russia, what were they and where *did* they come from? General Samford offered the theory that what had been picked up on radar were "ghosts" — or to put the matter in somewhat less sensational terms, false readings caused by hot weather conditions. The particular weather condition he mentioned was a temperature inversion, in which a pocket of cold air is trapped between layers of warm air. Since radar in 1952 was still relatively unsophisticated such a temperature inversion could create a *mirage*, or a false reading on radar. It had happened before, and radar operators were well aware of the effect.

The explanation sounded scientific enough. It was certainly good enough for *The New York Times*, where a front-page story was headlined: AIR FORCE DEBUNKS 'SAUCER' AS JUST 'NATURAL PHENOMENA.'

By this time, however, an awful lot of people just didn't believe anything the Air Force said. The UFO enthusiasts, who were now a large and well-organized movement in the United States, openly scoffed at such an explanation.

Yes, they admitted, temperature inversions could cause false radar readings. And yes, there were temperature inversions in the atmosphere above Washington on the two nights in July. But the inversions were not strong enough to produce all the effects that had been observed on those summer nights. Experienced radar operators who had been on duty those nights in July knew what weather phenomena looked like on radar. In fact, there had been weather-created targets on the radarscope at the time the "unknowns" appeared. The unknowns were different. They appeared to represent solid objects.

The newsmen weren't convinced. A United Press International reporter who had attended the packed news conference recalled, "It must be said . . . that there are persons intimately involved in the

July episode, with the events of those ten days still blazing in memory like meteors, who regard the temperature-inversion explanation as no explanation."

Even Captain Ruppelt, who was, after all, supposed to be the Air Force's top UFO investigator, was unconvinced by this explanation. He wrote: "On each night that there was a sighting there was a temperature inversion, but it was never strong enough to affect the radar in the way inversions normally do. On each occasion I checked the strength of the inversion according to the methods used by the Air Defense Command Weather Forecast Center." Project Blue Book independently investigated the incidents and continued to list the cause of the Washington National Airport sightings as "unknown."

It's no wonder that back in the 1950s so many people felt that something really big was going on — and they weren't being told the truth about it.

CHAPTER SIX

Swamp Gas

Early in the morning of September 3, 1965, something large, luminous, and very mysterious was seen hovering around the little town of Exeter, New Hampshire.

At 12:30 A.M. Patrolman Eugene Bertrand was hailed by a woman parked alongside Route 101, just beyond the city limits. She was very excited. She said that her car had been followed by a large, glowing object. She pointed to a bright light on the horizon. It was a long distance away now, and to Bertrand it looked like a bright star; it didn't look unusual or menacing. He reassured the woman, didn't even bother to take her name, and forgot about the incident — for about an hour and a half.

At 2 A.M. the patrolman got a call to come to headquarters to investigate the claim of a young man who said he had seen a UFO. Eighteen-year-old Norman Muscarello was hitchhiking back to his home in Exeter from a nearby town. He was standing on Route 150 about two miles (three kilometers) outside the town when a large, roundish object with four or five bright red lights on it rose out of the nearby woods. It silently moved over a field and to a nearby farmhouse where it hovered for a short time just a few feet (about a meter) above the roof. Then it moved off over the field and disappeared behind the trees. Muscarello estimated that the thing was about ninety feet (twenty-seven meters) in diameter.

He pounded on the door of the house, shouting that he had seen a flying saucer. The residents thought he was drunk and wouldn't let him in. Muscarello then flagged down a passing car and was driven to the police station.

It was a pale and badly shaken young man who blurted out his strange tale to the police. He wasn't drunk and didn't appear to be crazy. That's why Bertrand was contacted. He was told to take Muscarello back to the place where he had sighted the UFO and investigate.

When they arrived at the scene there was nothing to see. After waiting a few minutes they went into the field near the house for a closer look. Bertrand was examining the ground with his flashlight when Muscarello began shouting that the thing had come back. And there it was, rising slowly from behind some nearby trees.

Bertrand described it as a large, dark object with a straight row of bright red lights that dimmed from right to left and left to right, alternately. The object seemed to be coming straight for them. Bertrand drew his gun, but on second thought figured that was useless. Instead he rushed back to his car and radioed headquarters. Within a few minutes Officer David Hunt arrived. The three watched the object move soundlessly back over the trees and disappear.

A few minutes later police headquarters received a call from a man who said that he was in a phone booth and a UFO was heading straight for him. Then the line went dead. The caller was never identified.

A number of possible explanations for these sightings were offered. They ranged from experimental aircraft being tested at a nearby Air Force base to distortions of stars and planets caused by temperature inversions. Philip Klass, an aviation writer who was to become the most persistent and outspoken UFO skeptic, said they were glowing electrical discharges from nearby power lines. Others suggested they were natural phenomena like the northern lights.

The main witnesses were unimpressed by such explanations. So was the public at large. Suddenly UFOs were back.

By the mid-1960s the excitement of the early days of flying saucers had died down. The number of sightings had dropped off significantly. To many of us who had been in at the start of the excitement, it appeared that the Age of Flying Saucers was over. Boy, were we ever wrong!

The Exeter sightings rekindled interest in the subject. But what really blew the lid off the whole UFO story in the 1960s was a series of incidents that took place in Michigan during March of 1966.

The sightings started on March 14 near the city of Ann Arbor. A large number of people saw strange glowing objects in the predawn sky. On March 17 another crowd saw a similar event over another part of the same Michigan county.

Perhaps the most impressive sightings in this series took place on March 20. The setting was a swampy area near Dexter, a small town some ten miles (sixteen kilometers) west of Ann Arbor. At about 8:30 P.M. a local farmer named Frank Mannor and his son Ronald said they saw a bright object drop out of the sky and land about half a mile (one kilometer) from their farm. At first they thought it was a meteor. They said that they got to within 500 yards (450 meters) of the object, which clearly wasn't a meteor because it was hovering over the swamp flashing red and blue lights.

After the Mannors reported the incident, a small crowd gathered quickly and watched several objects of this type. The elusive objects were also chased by at least six patrol cars.

The grand finale took place the following night at Hillsdale, twenty miles (thirty-two kilometers) west of Dexter. Hillsdale civil defense director William

Van Horn, a college dean, and eighty-seven women from Hillsdale College watched for several hours as a huge UFO with flashing lights hovered over a nearby swamp. These witnesses all stayed a safe distance from whatever it was out there.

The Michigan sightings generated a tremendous amount of publicity. A few days later Major Hector Quintanilla, who was then the head of the Air Force's Project Blue Book, arrived on the scene for an investigation. Captain Ruppelt, who had been head of Blue Book in the early 1950s, had retired from the Air Force. He died in 1960. Along with Quintanilla was Dr. J. Allen Hynek, a professor of astronomy at Northwestern University and the chief scientific consultant for Project Blue Book.

The two made a quick examination of the scenes at Dexter and Hillsdale, and talked to some of the witnesses. And then, on March 25, the Air Force quickly called a press conference. Dr. Hynek was shocked. At that point he had no idea what the people of Michigan had seen. He protested to the Air Force. It did no good. Later he complained, "I was to have a press conference ready or not."

Since the sightings had already received wide attention, the hotel room in which the press conference was held was jammed with reporters and photographers. And they were all shouting questions at Dr. Hynek. He had never been in this situation before and he felt under tremendous pressure. "Searching for a possible explanation of the sightings I remembered a phone call from a botanist at the University of Michigan who had called to my attention the phenomenon of burning swamp gas. . . . After learning more about swamp gas from other Michigan scientists I decided that it was a 'possible' explanation that I would offer to reporters."

It was a big mistake, and Hynek knew it almost immediately. Though the room did not actually erupt in laughter, there were skeptical noises coming from the crowd.

Major Quintanilla made matters worse when he said that he was perfectly satisfied with the swamp gas theory and was going to place the Michigan sightings in the "explained" category. Officially, Project Blue Book was stuck with "swamp gas."

When the story was broadcast and printed a lot of people did laugh out loud. But some of those who had seen the UFOs were angry. They were sure they had been looking at solid craft with arrays of flashing lights. Now they were being told that what they had really seen was swamp gas. It was downright insulting. Neither Dr. Hynek nor Major Quintanilla had been there to see what they had seen.

Patrolman Robert Hunawill, a witness at the Dexter sightings, summed up the feelings of many: "It's not swamp gas! My reaction to Dr. Hynek is the same as the rest of the people around here. He made us look like fools. I don't think he'll get any cooperation out of these people anymore."

The general public thought it was Dr. Hynek and

the Air Force that looked like fools. Overwhelmingly people felt that it was the explanation, not the UFOs, that was swamp gas. Comedians made jokes about swamp gas. For a long time the term *swamp gas* came to mean any half-baked and unsupportable explanation or excuse. Besides, the words *swamp gas* just sound funny.

To those already convinced that the government was engaged in a massive UFO cover-up the story looked like just another part — although a rather silly one — of the conspiracy of silence, the conspiracy to cover up the truth about UFOs.

In reality, the theory isn't as dumb as it sounds at first. Rotting vegetation in marshes and swamps *does* produce quantities of methane gas — popularly called marsh gas or swamp gas. Sometimes, when a large quantity of gas is released at once, it can ignite and become luminous. Just how and why this happens no one is quite sure — but it does happen. The phenomenon known as will-o'-the-wisp, fox fire, jack-o'-lantern, and other names is luminous swamp gas. In some places these flickering lights were regarded with dread because they were supposed to be spirits who led unwary travelers astray in swamps or actual omens of death.

The Michigan UFOs appeared in the right place for swamp gas — over swamps — and at the right time of year — early spring, when large quantities of gas can be released after the ice melts. So the explanation that Dr. Hynek gave was possible. All he ever said was that it was "possible."

But what the witnesses reported did not behave like luminous swamp gas usually does. For example, bubbles of luminous swamp gas are rarely larger than four or five feet (120–150 centimeters) across. What was seen in Michigan was twenty or more feet (six or more meters) in diameter. Swamp gas generally hovers just a few feet (about a meter) in the air. Yet in Michigan the luminous things were seen to rise a couple of hundred feet (about sixty meters). Finally, pockets of luminous swamp gas are not known to last nearly as long as what people in Michigan saw those March evenings.

So the Michigan sightings could have been swamp gas. But they probably weren't.

The whole incident was particularly painful for Dr. Allen Hynek. He was the Northwestern University astronomer who had been chief scientific consultant for the Air Force UFO project for many years. It was his job to try to explain UFO sightings. Many of those who believed that UFOs were spaceships regarded Hynek as the Prince of Darkness, chief spokesman for the conspiracy of silence. After the swamp gas episode he looked less like a conspirator and more like a fool.

In fact, Hynek was a well-trained astronomer who had been in charge of tracking the first artificial satellites. He was very open-minded. Over the years that he had spent investigating UFOs, he had become more and more convinced that there was *something* — he was never sure what — behind the phenomena; that not all UFO sightings were mistakes, hoaxes, or swamp gas. A few years after the great swamp gas fiasco Dr. Hynek publicly announced his belief in UFOs. It was a startling announcement. All of those in the UFO world who had thought of him as the enemy had to start thinking of him as a friend.

After he retired Hynek became the chief scientific spokesman *for* UFOs. He wrote several books on the subject and founded a UFO investigation organization that still exists today. He was also a consultant for Steven Spielberg's classic UFO film *Close Encounters of the Third Kind*. Hynek even makes a brief appearance in the film.

After the swamp gas episode public suspicion that the Air Force either was hiding something about UFOs or simply didn't know what it was doing reached new heights. There were calls in Congress for a broader investigation.

One of those pressing hardest for a new investigation was the congressman from the Michigan district where the sightings took place. He also happened to be Republican minority leader in the U.S. House of Representatives. His name was Gerald Ford. In September 1974 Ford was to become president of the United States after the resignation of Richard Nixon.

UFOs, which appeared to be on their way out, were back — with a vengeance.

CHAPTER SEVEN

Close Encounters of the Third Kind

It was the astronomer and former Air Force consultant J. Allen Hynek who developed the classification system for UFO encounters.

A close encounter of the first kind was seeing a UFO.

A close encounter of the second kind was seeing the occupants in the UFO.

A close encounter of the third kind was meeting with occupants face-to-face.

There is a close encounter of the fourth kind, but that's for the next chapter.

What has been called the "grandaddy of all occupant sightings" took place on August 21, 1955, near Hopkinsville, Kentucky.

Chief of Police Russell Greenwell went to bed early that night, but just before midnight he was awakened by a phone call from headquarters. The voice over the phone sounded excited: "Chief, you had better get down here. We've got a couple of carloads of nearly hysterical people. And they're all telling the craziest story."

The chief was still groggy when he got to the station. What he heard there woke him up completely.

The whole thing had started some four hours earlier at a farmhouse occupied by Mrs. Lenny Langford, her son Cecil "Lucky" Sutton, and his family. The old-style house was located about eight miles (thirteen kilometers) outside of Hopkinsville and about half a mile (a kilometer) from the main highway. It was a fairly isolated spot.

The Suttons had visitors at the time so there were a lot of people in the house, seven or eight adults and several children. At the police station everybody was talking at once, so the exact sequence of events is not clear. But basically, here is what they said happened: Shortly after 7 P.M. one of the people in the house was looking out the back door when he heard a hissing sound and saw a bright light come out of the sky. The light appeared to settle on the ground a few hundred yards (a few hundred meters) from the house.

The adults went out to investigate. Before they could get very far they saw several little men coming toward the house. They were strange and frightening-looking creatures.

They were about three and one half feet (106 centimeters) tall with roundish heads, huge elephantlike ears, and slitlike mouths. Their eyes were outsized, even for their outsized heads, and set very wide apart. The arms of the creatures hung nearly to the ground and ended in clawlike appendages. They seemed to be wearing silvery garments. According to one witness, the things floated rather than walked. According to another they ran, and when they did they dropped to all fours.

Some of the men reacted instinctively and grabbed their guns, though no threatening moves had been made by the strange visitors. Lucky Sutton got his shotgun; guest Billy Ray Taylor grabbed a 22-caliber target pistol. They went inside the house and waited. . . . They didn't have long to wait.

One of the strange, big-eared heads popped up at the window. Sutton fired his shotgun at point-blank range — right through the screen. The blast should have shattered anything outside. But the little man seemed relatively unharmed. The shot knocked the creature over, but it scuttled away on all fours.

As Taylor stepped out the back door, he heard Sutton shout, "Look out! He's trying to get you." A creature had climbed onto the low roof of the house and reached over to make a grab for Taylor's hair or head. Taylor managed to shake himself free of its grasp.

After that things really got confusing. The creatures seemed to be climbing all over the house. They were also up in the trees. The men went around shooting at them, without much effect. The little men didn't actually hurt anybody. But they didn't seem capable of being hurt, either.

After nearly four hours the creatures were still not frightened off. But the people in the house were scared to death. If the alien creatures weren't going to leave, the humans would. They piled into two cars and headed for Hopkinsville and the police station.

Chief Greenwell listened to this story with growing amazement. The witnesses were excited, confused, and not making much sense, but they were genuinely scared.

Crazy as the story sounded, Chief Greenwell decided it was worth investigating. By this time the Hopkinsville police had been joined by the state police and the county sheriff's office. They all went out to the farm and searched as thoroughly as they could in the dark. They found nothing. If a flying saucer had landed at Mrs. Langford's place, it was gone before the police arrived. There were no marks to indicate that any sort of craft had ever landed and no signs of any strange footprints; indeed, there was not a single piece of visible evidence that anything unusual had taken place, except for a big hole in one window screen. That was where Lucky Sutton had discharged his shotgun at the alien face.

There was no one to arrest and nothing to do.

Chief Greenwell and his men went home. But the chief couldn't get the incident out of his mind. The next morning he was back at the farmhouse. The people were still frightened and excited. They said that the alien creatures had returned at about 3:30 in the morning. One or more of them was peering through the window. Sutton took another shot, and he showed the chief another bullet hole in the screen. But a thorough investigation of the area, this time in daylight, turned up no additional evidence.

Still most of those who came to the scene felt quite sure *something* had happened. No one knew what.

The Hopkinsville shootout made national news and attracted reporters and curiosity seekers from a wide area. After poking around, most investigators concluded that the Sutton family had a generally good reputation. Some who knew them thought that they were rather excitable folk, but no one thought that they were the sort of people who would try to pull off an elaborate hoax, nor were they the sort of people who habitually reported "seeing things."

One suggestion was that they had all succumbed to mass hysteria. But what could have made them hysterical in the first place?

A few days after the event Mrs. Langford and the Sutton family picked up and left the area. This started a flood of rumors that the witnesses had been kidnapped, either by the space aliens themselves or by some secret government agency trying to hide the truth about flying saucers. In fact, their departure was quite unsensational. They just got fed up with the attention. A lot of people had been calling them liars, or just plain crazy. They wanted to get away from all of that.

A year after the incident an investigator tracked down those who had been involved in the Hopkinsville shootout. They stuck to their original accounts, but could add nothing new.

The Hopkinsville incident was so weird that no one knew what to make of it. The Socorro landing, on the other hand, was more prosaic and therefore more believable. It is a classic close encounter.

Policeman Lonnie Zamora, of Socorro, New Mexico, was just doing his job on April 24, 1964. At about 5:45 in the afternoon he saw a car zooming down the highway, far exceeding the speed limit. He took off after it. That was his job.

Just outside of town he heard and saw something that made him break off his chase. There was a roar and flash of light in the southwest. Officer Zamora knew there were some shacks in the area in which dynamite was stored. He feared there had been an explosion and decided to investigate.

Officer Zamora turned off the highway and headed down a rough gravel road in the direction of the dynamite shacks. He had just come over a steep hill when out to the west he spotted what at first looked like a car turned upside down. Standing nearby were two figures in white overalls. One of them looked straight at the policeman and seemed to jump in surprise. The figures looked fully human but quite short, like children.

Zamora drove nearer to the object to get a better look. He briefly lost sight of it as he passed behind another hill. When he could see it again he was much closer and realized that it was not a car. What he saw was an "aluminum-white," egg-shaped object standing on four girderlike legs. There was a peculiar red insignia on the side. It looked something like an arrow pointing up from a horizontal base to a semicircular crown. Zamora had never seen anything like the object or the insignia before.

He grabbed the microphone on his car radio and reported to headquarters that he would be getting out of his car to check an apparent accident scene. The message was also received by State Patrolman Sam Chavez. Chavez immediately set out to help Zamora but he took a wrong turn and was late in arriving.

As Zamora made the call the two figures had disappeared. Officer Zamora got out of his car and started walking toward the object. He heard two or three loud thumps, "like someone possibly hammering, or shutting a door or doors hard." The object then began emitting an ominous roar, and

Officer Zamora could see a flame under it. Fearing the thing was about to explode, he began to run back toward his patrol car. He tried to look behind while running and in his excitement actually bumped into the patrol car and knocked off his glasses.

The policeman kept on running until the roar stopped. He then turned around to look, covering his face with his arms, just in case there was an explosion. The object had lifted off the ground. The flame had disappeared and the roar changed to a low whine that lasted for just a few seconds — and then there was complete silence. The object moved off toward the southwest, hovering ten to fifteen feet (three to five meters) above the ground. It picked up speed as it went and finally it disappeared from view.

With the thing gone, Zamora recovered a bit. He returned to the patrol car and retrieved his glasses. He was able to see that the dry brush where the object had been standing was now ablaze.

Patrolman Zamora then got back on the radio and called headquarters again. He told the radio operator to "look out the window, to see if you can see an object."

Just a few seconds later Sergeant Chavez arrived. He found a pale and badly shaken Zamora, who was pointing excitedly to the burning area. The two policemen walked over to the spot where the fire had already begun to die out. Chavez pointed out four squarish imprints in the ground, possibly where the legs of the craft had rested. He also saw several small, shallow, circular imprints that were later described as footprints or perhaps imprints made by a ladder.

As soon as Lonnie Zamora's story became known it created a sensation. Reporters and folks who were interested in UFOs flocked to the small New Mexico town to talk to the patrolman and to visit the place where he said he saw the strange craft take off.

This UFO landing case is still generally regarded as one of the best on record. The big problem is that the only person who saw the craft and its two occupants was Zamora himself. Everyone else in the area was asked if they had seen a strange craft on April 24, 1964. No one said they had.

However, Opel Grinder, a Socorro gas station attendant, was told by a motorist that he had seen a silvery craft flying low over the highway at about the same time Zamora made his sighting. Years later investigators tracked down a man named Larry Kratzer. Kratzer and his passenger, Paul Kles, recalled driving through Socorro on April 24, 1964, and seeing a silvery object and a cloud of smoke about a mile (more than a kilometer) ahead of them on the highway. They also vaguely remembered mentioning this to a gas station attendant.

Later they heard reports of the Zamora sighting on the car radio. That made them think twice about what they might have seen at Socorro. When they got home to Dubuque, Iowa, they told their story to a local newspaper reporter. But he wrote a garbled account.

Most of those who interviewed Zamora thought he was an honest witness who wasn't just making up the story to get publicity. He had a good record as a policeman and a reputation for truthfulness among his friends and neighbors. Dr. Allen Hynek, chief scientific consultant for the government's Project Blue Book, came out to talk to Zamora and was very impressed, though he wasn't sure what the patrolman had actually seen.

Perhaps what Zamora saw wasn't really a space-ship from another world. It has been suggested that he saw a secret U.S. military craft being tested. The two figures in the white coveralls were described as looking fully human, though small in stature. There was a large military base in the Socorro area. In fact, Larry Kratzer at first thought that what he had seen was a secret Air Force experimental craft.

The Air Force, however, has vigorously denied that it was testing any secret craft around Socorro. The Air Force went even further by insisting that it had never tested anything that looked like what Lonnie Zamora said he saw — anywhere, ever. In the years since the Socorro sighting no evidence has come to light to indicate that the sighting was caused by a secret military project.

Of course, there are those who think Zamora just made the whole thing up because he wanted the attention.

In the end, like so many other reported UFO encounters of the last fifty years, the one at Socorro remains unexplained, controversial, and very intriguing.

CHAPTER EIGHT
Abducted

Since the beginning of the Age of Flying Saucers there has always been an argument over whether space aliens are friendly or unfriendly. In 1961 a New Hampshire couple added a whole new dimension to that argument. Their story indicated that not only were the aliens *un*friendly, they were likely to reach out and grab you right off the street. That is a close encounter of the fourth kind and it's not the kind of encounter anyone wants to have.

When their story became widely known a few years later the Age of the Abductee had begun, and it's still with us. People had reported being taken aboard UFOs before. There was Dan Fry, who said he was given a nice, friendly ride aboard one of the alien spaceships. Then there was the well-publicized case of Antonio Villas Boas, a young Brazilian farmer who, in 1957, told of being captured by aliens and assaulted by an alien woman "much more beautiful than any woman I have ever known" before being released.

But such stories were for the contactee lunatic fringe or the sensation-mongering supermarket tabloids. They were not taken seriously by serious UFO buffs. What happened to Betty and Barney Hill in 1961 was completely different.

In the first place the Hills were not obvious lunatics nor were they self-promoters. On the contrary, they were deeply troubled by what they believed had happened to them and had never sought publicity.

On the night of September 19, 1961, the Hills were returning to their home in Portsmouth, New Hampshire, from a vacation in Canada. They were driving on Route 3, through a nearly uninhabited area when, around midnight, they thought they were being followed by a bright object in the sky. They stopped the car several times to look at it through binoculars. Then the object seemed to come around in front of the car and hover above the road. At first Barney thought it was a military helicopter. They could see humanoid figures in shiny black uniforms inside the craft. At this point they became very frightened because the craft didn't look like a helicopter anymore. It was clearly alien. They now felt trapped. "Like a bug in a net," Barney said.

The next thing they remember, they were again driving down the road. When they looked back there was no UFO. It was about two hours later than it should have been, and they figured they were about thirty-five miles (fifty-six kilometers) from the place where they had seen the UFO.

After they got home, both the Hills began to suffer from acute anxiety and a variety of physical complaints, some quite severe. Betty had nightmares about their car being stopped by a group of men wearing military-type uniforms, and then being taken aboard a strange disk-shaped craft.

The symptoms grew worse over the next two years. Their own doctor could find no physical reason for the distress. On his advice the Hills consulted psychiatrist Dr. Benjamin Simon. Dr. Simon hypnotized Betty and Barney separately in an attempt to bring back what might be repressed memories of the events of the lost two hours of that September 1961 night.

They each told a similar story about being taken aboard a UFO and given physical examinations and tests. The experience was not a pleasant one. Up close the abductors were distinctly nonhuman in appearance. They had the oversized heads and insectlike faces that have now become the standard picture of a space alien.

Betty recalled being able to communicate with the aliens. They did not seem to be evil, merely indifferent. Both Betty and Barney felt as if they were treated more like laboratory specimens than human beings.

Betty asked the apparent leader where he was from. He showed her a star map. Betty was able to redraw the map under hypnosis. The map became the source of a major controversy in the UFO community. Some people thought the map represented the area near the stars Zeta 1 and Zeta 2 Reticuli. According to this interpretation the stars shown on the map were all basically like the sun and could theoretically have planets like Earth. Critics, however, think Betty Hill's star map is just a random grouping of dots and lines, that have been interpreted too broadly.

After the alien examination the Hills were released, and told that they would not remember what had happened to them. And they didn't — at least until they were hypnotized by Dr. Simon.

There was no doubt in Dr. Simon's mind, and in the minds of many others who met the Hills, that they *believed* they were telling the truth. But hypnotized subjects don't automatically tell the truth — that is, give a description of what actually happened. They can report a fantasy as truth if they believe that fantasy to be true. The whole subject of memories recovered through hypnosis is very controversial among those who study the workings of the human mind.

The Hills were, at first, rather embarrassed about the whole incident. All they wanted to do was get rid of the headaches, insomnia, and other symptoms that seemed to be a direct result of their encounter. But the story was so incredible that they did talk about it with friends, and word of the abduction got around. The Hill case came to the attention of writer John Fuller who had been researching a book on the Exeter, New Hampshire, UFO sightings. With the cooperation of the Hills and the psychiatrist Fuller wrote a book called *Interrupted Journey*. The 1996 publication of the book coincided with a lot of other UFO activity, like the Michigan sightings (chapter six). It became a best-seller and one of the most influential UFO books ever written. It was also made into a first-rate TV movie.

The attention the Hill case received opened the door to a huge number of other abduction stories. People were practically coming out of the woodwork, insisting that they, too, had been kidnapped by aliens.

One case that got a good deal of attention was the tale told by Calvin Parker and Charles Hickson of Pascagoula, Mississippi. The two men said that on October 11, 1973, they had been fishing when they saw a bright object descend behind them. As the craft settled, they saw three creatures get out and move in their direction.

Even in the world of space aliens these creatures were strange-looking. They were about five feet (152 centimeters) tall with very wrinkled pale gray skin. They didn't have any neck, the head coming down on the shoulders. There were two small conelike ears, slits where the eyes should be, and a small sharp nose with holes below it. The arms ended in clawlike hands with only two fingers each. The legs seemed to be fused together, and they moved by floating.

The two men were so terrified by the sight they couldn't move. In a paralyzed state they were "floated" aboard the UFO, examined with a large "eyelike" device, and then floated out of the vehicle and left on the riverbank. The creatures floated back into their craft, and the craft took off and disappeared into the night sky.

The two men were shaken and were worried that people would not believe them and would laugh at them. But after calming down, they went first to the local newspaper office. It was closed, so they went to the sheriff's office.

The two men claimed they didn't want any publicity, but they immediately hired a lawyer, and within twenty-four hours the story got out and they were world famous.

What followed was a confused, confusing, and sometimes comical series of events. The two Mississippi fishermen, as they were called, were interviewed by some of the country's leading UFO researchers, including Dr. J. Allen Hynek. Hynek was convinced they had experienced some sort of frightening experience, though he didn't know if it had anything to do with alien spaceships. The newspapers weren't as reserved. One headline read: SCIENTISTS BELIEVE MEN AND UFO STORY.

The men then took a lie detector test, which they

passed. That was big news. But the lie detector isn't infallible and this test certainly wasn't. The man who gave the test had never even completed the training course in operating the device. When police offered to give them another lie detector test — this one administered by one of the country's top experts — they agreed, but then backed out at the last minute.

There were also a lot of holes in the story, which seemed to change a bit every time it was told. For instance, there was a busy highway near the spot where the two fishermen claimed to have been abducted. No one else saw the brightly lighted spaceship that night. Soon even die-hard UFO believers were becoming suspicious and discouraged.

The Travis Walton case appeared much more promising — at first. On November 5, 1975, six young woodcutters and their employer were working in the Apache-Sitgreaves National Forest in east central Arizona.

At about 6:00 in the evening they were in a truck heading home along a forest road. They saw what appeared to be a large glowing object hovering about fifteen feet (five meters) above a clearing in the forest. The truck stopped and one of the men, Travis Walton, jumped out to get a closer look. As he neared the object a beam of light shot out and seemed to lift him right off the ground. The driver of the truck panicked and began to drive away. As the truck began to move, the object rose from the ground and quickly disappeared over the horizon. The driver then turned the truck around and drove back to the clearing where the men began to search for Walton. They couldn't find any trace of him. His disappearance was reported to the police.

At midnight five days later Walton called his sister. He sounded confused and disoriented, and said he was in terrible pain. He told his sister that he was calling from a phone booth in the nearby town of Heber. Walton gave the location of the phone booth and then hung up. His brother and brother-in-law drove to Heber, where they found Travis in the phone booth, unconscious. He had a five-day growth of beard, but once he awoke he appeared uninjured.

Ultimately Walton was hypnotized, but was able to recall only a small part of the missing five days. He said that he had been inside of some sort of hospital-like room and was stretched out on what appeared to be an examination table. Around the table were three strange creatures: small, each with a large domed head, large eyes, and small nose and mouth. Each was encased in a tan, seamless jumpsuit.

Walton also reported seeing a tall man with brown hair and strange golden-brown eyes who led him around to various rooms containing objects and apparatus that he could not recognize. He met several other humanoid beings who managed to place an apparatus resembling an oxygen mask over his face. He then lost consciousness.

He woke up in the desert near Heber. He awoke just in time to see the curved metallic hull of the spaceship take off straight up into the air and disappear. After that he stumbled into town, found the phone booth, and called his sister.

Walton could provide no other evidence of his abduction. There was a widespread suspicion in the ufological community that the whole thing was a rather elaborate hoax, though this was never proved. His book, *The Walton Experience*, sold briskly, and a film based on the book had a modest success. Those who took UFOs seriously, however, never took the Travis Walton case very seriously.

Far more influential were what came to be called the "missing time" cases. The Hills believed that they could not account for about two hours during which they had been abducted by space aliens, taken aboard a UFO, given an often painful physical examination, and then released with no memory, or at best a very fuzzy and incomplete one, of what had happened to them. The experience had created serious physical and psychological problems for them. The details of what had happened to them were only recalled under hypnosis years later.

After the Hill case became well known, hundreds and perhaps thousands of people began reporting similar missing-time experiences. Many of them were hypnotized and recalled similar abduction experiences.

Typical of these was the experience reported by Sandy Larson, her fifteen-year-old daughter Jackie, and Jackie's boyfriend Terry O'Leary. They were driving down the road toward Bismarck, North Dakota, on the morning of August 26, 1975, when they saw eight to ten UFOs hovering over a grove of trees twenty yards (eighteen meters) away. Then the witnesses had an odd sensation of being "frozen" or "stuck" for a second or two after which they saw the UFOs flying away. But now Jackie, who had been sitting in the middle of the front seat was in the back seat, with no idea how she had gotten there. And it was an hour later than it should have been.

A few months after the experience Sandy Larson and her daughter were hypnotized. Sandy recalled being floated into a UFO. A six-foot-tall (182 centimeters) robotlike creature with glaring eyes put her on a table, rubbed a clear liquid over her, and inserted an instrument up her nose. After a time she and Terry (who did not recall seeing the inside of the UFO) were returned to the car, and all conscious memory of the incident had vanished.

The science-fiction and horror-story writer Whitley Streiber reported that two days after Christmas 1985 he had been abducted from the bedroom of his house in New York State. Under hypnosis he told the now familiar story of being floated into a UFO and given a thorough and sometimes painful physical examination by the big-headed, gray-skinned, bug-eyed creatures, then being floated back to the spot from which he had been taken with no conscious memory of what had happened.

In later hypnotic sessions Streiber told of contacts with aliens since his childhood and of seeing both his father and sister on examination tables inside the UFO. It all sounds like an *X-Files* plot. In fact, Streiber wrote an enormously successful book called *Communion* about his experience. For a brief period Streiber was a national celebrity.

Streiber wrote a couple of other books that expand on his alien contacts. In 1993, however, he confessed that he had never been abducted by aliens. He then took back the confession and said he *had* been abducted, and . . . well, the whole thing became so confused and contradictory that nobody paid much attention to him anymore.

But bizarre and even unbelievable as these abduction stories may sound, they have left us with a very uncomfortable feeling.

CHAPTER NINE

What Is Going On Here?

It seemed so simple back in the late 1940s and early 1950s. The flying saucer would land in some obvious place, like the middle of Washington, D.C. The door would slide open and a space alien, perhaps looking like Michael Rennie from *The Day the Earth Stood Still*, would step out, wave, and say, "I come in peace." And all our problems would be solved.

Or — to take the less optimistic view — a space alien, looking like a gigantic insect, would step out and say something like "Resistance is futile." And our problems would just be starting.

Failing either of these two extreme alternatives, the flying saucers or the UFOs would just fade away. We would look back on the era as some sort of historical curiosity and marvel at how naive and foolish we had all been to believe in such things back then when we were young.

The problem is that none of the above has happened. The flying saucers certainly have not landed, but they have not gone away, either. They are still there, tantalizing and confusing us.

It is this elusiveness that has led many in the ufological world to frustration, despair, and some wild-eyed theorizing that borders on absolute nuttiness. We begin talking about things like "high strangeness," which means the weirder, the more unbelievable the UFO report is the more likely it is to be true.

Many of us become Fox Mulder without a Dana Scully trying to bring us back to some sort of commonsense reality. And if you think some of the things you have heard on the *X-Files* are strange, just wait till you hear what UFO buffs have proposed — and seriously, too.

Some people have suggested that UFOs really started with that old science-fiction magazine editor Ray Palmer. Certainly some of the strangest UFO theories started with Palmer. Talk about open-minded! He was ready for anything.

Even before UFOs, Palmer had been promoting the theories of a man named Richard S. Shaver. Shaver believed, or at least said he believed, that Earth was hollow and the interior was inhabited by creatures he called "detrimental robots" or "deros." The deros caused most of the world's troubles by controlling people's minds with rays projected from their underground caverns.

At first the Shaver stories were presented as fiction in Palmer's magazines, but then the editor began receiving letters from people claiming that they, too, had had experiences with the deros, and that Shaver was telling the truth. After that Palmer began presenting the Shaver underground world stories as fact.

When flying saucers came along, Palmer abandoned the underground world for the more exciting realms of outer space. But later in his career Palmer decided that the flying saucers did not come from outer space at all, but from the inside of Shaver's hollow Earth. They entered our atmosphere through large holes in the North and South Poles.

You didn't know that there are huge holes in the North and South Poles that are gateways to the hollow Earth? When Earth-orbiting satellites first began taking pictures of the planet, there were those who insisted the photos showed the polar holes clearly but that the evidence was literally being covered-up by the government. (I was shown several unretouched photos of Earth with big holes at the poles. But that is a story for another day.)

Palmer's saucers from the hollow earth never really caught on, though there was more serious discussion of the subject in ufological circles than one might imagine. Suggestions that the UFOs came from secret undersea bases (the products of an underwater rather than other-worldly civilization) or bases on the dark side of the moon never gained many followers.

More popular was the theory that UFOs did not first appear in 1947, but have, in one form or another, always been with us. These theories were popularized by Erich Von Däniken, a Swiss hotel manager turned author. Starting in 1968 with *Chariots of the Gods*, Von Däniken produced a string of books on what has been called the Ancient Astronaut theory. Over a short period of time his books sold tens of millions of copies worldwide, making him one of the most successful and widely read authors in history.

Von Däniken said that the gods of ancient times were really space aliens, who helped to shape our civilization. He also said that these gods were not necessarily friendly and that we should do everything possible to prepare for their eventual return. The rash of UFO sightings just might have been the gods preparing the way for their return.

However, when others began to closely examine the evidence upon which Von Däniken based his Ancient Astronaut theories they found that much of it was misinterpreted, and some of it was downright fraudulent. Eventually the criticism affected Von Däniken's popularity, and Ancient Astronaut theories began to fade.

A fascinating theory is that the UFOs don't come from another planet — but do come from another time. The theory is based on the premise that humanity will advance to such a high technological level in the future that time travel will become commonplace. Naturally, people of the future will then wish to travel to the past to simply observe, or perhaps to manipulate, history. In any case they would probably disguise their intentions — perhaps by making us think that they came from space rather than from the future. This is a highly intriguing idea, but for some reason it never caught on.

Another fascinating theory that never caught on is that UFOs are not ships at all, but living things — space animals — that cruise the galaxies. Perhaps there is more than one type of these creatures, which is why there have been so many different descriptions of UFOs. But, as noted, this theory has few followers.

One of the most frustrating aspects of believing in UFOs is the lack of physical evidence. In over half a century of interest not a single undisputed piece of physical evidence of extraterrestrial visitation has ever been produced. It's not that evidence has not been offered — contactee Howard Menger produced a Lunar potato, which was supposed to have five times more protein than an ordinary Earth potato, and most recently there have been the supposed films of the autopsy of an alien creature's body. But I said no *undisputed* evidence.

This lack of physical evidence has led to what has been called the ultraterrestrial theory — that the UFOs come from some parallel universe or another dimension. In this theory, while the UFOs can be seen they don't really exist in our universe. The beauty of the theory is that there is no way of disproving it — on the other hand, there is no way of proving it, either.

Then there is the psychic projection theory. This holds that UFOs are projections of our collective unconscious. This theory is based on the work of psychiatrist Carl Jung. Now, while I have had the theory explained to me in great detail several times, I freely admit that I still don't understand it and I suspect that those who are doing the explaining don't understand it, either.

And there has been the suggestion that some secret earthly group has been projecting three-dimensional or holographic images of UFOs and their alien occupants to confuse us. It is all part of a grand deception to hide the true aims of this secret group. What the group is and what their aims are remain a mystery.

While these nonmaterial theories of UFOs have attracted a certain following in UFO circles, they have had almost no impact at all on the general public. Most people still think that UFOs are spaceships from other worlds, that the ships are being piloted by real, material alien creatures, and that one day, in their own good time, the aliens will set their ships down in Washington, D.C., or some other prominent location and announce once and for all, without any ambiguity or chance of misinterpretation, that they have arrived.